Murder Planet

By Adam Carpenter

Published By
Breaking Rules Publishing Europe

.

~ 2 ~

This is a work of fiction. Similarities to real people,
places, or events are
entirely coincidental.
MURDER PLANET
First edition. December 30, 2020.
Copyright © 2020 Adam Carpenter.
Written by Adam Carpenter.

~ 3 ~

Chapter 1

The sharp banging on the cell door woke Orton Bradshaw from a deep sleep.

"Wake up you scum!" he heard and the blissful ignorance that he enjoyed for a few seconds each morning disappeared.

"We're here!" the voice continued, "You have ten minutes to get your stuff in order and then you're taking the last flight of your lives!"

Bradshaw threw the blanket off him and quickly moved over to the toilet in his cell. As he did his business, he could see the sickly green and blue ball of Destitution out of the tiny window. The place where he was about to spend the rest of his life, however long that might be.

The door opened exactly nineteen minutes after the guard called out. Bradshaw straightened out his orange prison jumpsuit.

"Step forward, Bradshaw."

Orton did so, and the guard licked her lips... then spat in his face.

"I hope the drop bears kill you slowly, paedo."

She reached for the chains to restrain him on his final walk on a spaceship. Then a doctor came over, to give him an injection.

"It's an anti-malarial drug", he said, "There's a real problem with mosquitoes down there."

Another guard stood a short distance away, armed with a truncheon in case Bradshaw put up any resistance.

He didn't. There was no possibility of escape from this transport anyway. Not without killing multiple people and Orton Bradshaw, convicted of fourteen counts ranging from rape to witness tampering to distribution of child pornography, lacked the skills to kill multiple people. At least not without explosives.

The walk down to the pod bay was conducted in silence. In a small hall, an open hatch revealed the inside of a drop pod with five seats arrayed around a central console, its panels locked shut. Four of the five seats were occupied by other chained prisoners, all scary looking men. Two had tattoos, one had scars, the fourth had both. Bradshaw, a scrawny little man in his early 50s, would not stand a chance against one of them, let alone all of them.

He got inside and took his seat. One of the guards secured a four-point harness to keep him secure during what was to be a bumpy ride.

A shaven headed Hindu priest in a white robe started to read from a tablet in front of him.

Once the mantras had finished, the hatches were sealed, and a series of clunks followed as the magnetic locks were released. Then a slight jolt saw the drop pod pushed away from the prison transport.

* * * *

The spitting guard watched as the five people sentenced to life on the hellish rock below began their descent.

"Good riddance to bad rubbish", she said, "Now let's get out of here."

* * * *

Bradshaw's view out of the small window directly in his line of sight was of the prison transport moving away from them and the blackness of space.

At that point, a recording played.

"Prisoners. You have all been injected with a deadly virus. There are drugs that can counter-act this available at the research station that will be your new home, but they must be taken every day. All supplies will be sent down by pod. There is no way off the planet. Enjoy the rest of your life."

The other prisoners were confused at this. Bradshaw wondered how true this all was. The Bangla regime lied about so many things, why not this?

Bradshaw felt the retrorockets start to kick in. A display to his right showed their speed and height, both of which were starting to decrease as they commenced their re-entry. He knew the descent would be computer-controlled and while he could in theory take control of the craft, the fuel was limited on these pods to just a single descent.

Also, I don't know how to fly one of these things.

Outside, the sky started to glow as they began to enter the atmosphere. Things were getting bumpy now.

* * * *

Bradshaw tuned out the next few minutes until he felt the parachute deploy. All he could see was an increasingly blue sky anyway.

When they went vertical, he finally got his first proper look. A long carpet of green ran all its way to the horizon. It was probably trees. He hated trees.

The pod slowed down to a slow running pace as the landing legs deployed with the whirr of electrical motors and the clunks of them locking into place.

Then the final heavy bump as they landed.

"Might as well get out", one of the other prisoners, the one with scars and tattoo said. Bradshaw hadn't learned their names yet. Being in solitary confinement had limited his time for social interaction.

Scars and Tattoos unfastened his harness, moving over to the hatch and pulling the release handle to drop the boarding ramp. It fell to the ground with a thump and he started to walk down it.

Bradshaw saw him exit the ramp, step on a big flower... whose petals closed around his leg with a sharp chomp.

Scars and Tattoos would take four hours to die.

Chapter 2

Two weeks later in orbit around the independent world of New London, Bradshaw's potential salvation was about to face her latest challenge.

The sun rose for the tenth time that day as the merchant ship *Tulyar* completed another orbit and Sunita Kumar was briefly dazzled before the filters on the window kicked in to reduce the glare to a safe level. Below, the dark grey swirl indicated a storm was about to hit Plaistow City and she was grateful she'd drawn the shipboard duty rather than dealing with the unloading operations of their cargo on the surface of New London.

Then she was interrupted by a loud piercing wail, guaranteed to communicate to anyone in the room that there was a problem with its producer that needed dealing with.

She turned around and saw her six-month-old daughter, Kimberley, screaming in distress. Her nose picked up the reason instantly and she moved over to comfort the red-haired small human that was the major focus of her life right now. She figured out the reason instantly; well, the smell was instantly recognisable.

"Now, now, Kimmy," she said, "Don't worry, Mummy's going to change your nappy."

Picking up the baby from the crib where she'd previously been happily playing with her toy rabbit, Sunita walked over to the bathroom that now served as Baby Changing Central and reflected for the three hundredth time how she hadn't exactly planned this situation.

It was the norm in the world of the Spacees ('Spacers' if you were being formal and People of the Stellar Way if you were being *very* formal), the descendants of the nomadic peoples of Earth, to get married in your late teens and have your first child in your early twenties. With the shorter than average life expectancy of those exposed to the ravages of space, you made sure your DNA was replicated before it had a chance to mutate too much and produce cancers in unpleasant places; or before you had a helmet failure during a repair EVA.

"Don't cry, *bacha*, you'll be nice and fresh soon..."

Sunita Kumar was 23 and the brown-skinned face currently looking back at her in the mirror was closer to

30. She hadn't planned Kimmy; she'd not wanted a child until she'd gotten her second sleeve stripe. A drunken night with her husband, the *one time* that they'd not used protection, they had gotten six numbers in the pregnancy lottery and now she was going to have to wipe the result's bottom.

Placing her daughter on the changing table, she admired the screaming infant for a second. Dressed in a miniature version of the blue jumpsuit Sunita herself was wearing, she looked adorable. The copper hair mixed with the light brown skin tone and round face made her easy to spot; Kimmy's father, Daniel O'Hanlon, was of Irish descent.

She's so lovely... and yet so much of a challenge.

She was just reaching to remove Kimmy's jumpsuit when the intercom on her help buzzed. Her hand stopped in mid motion and she instead pressed a button to take the call.

"Go for Quartermaster Kumar..." she said, not even hiding her annoyance at the interruption. She was off duty and the rules for interruption were quite clear on this ship.

"Kumar, it's Security Officer Benson," came a female voice, "We've got a serious problem down on the surface and we need all the shipboard officers in the Map Room, immediately."

"Is this really immediate, Jessica? I'm busy now with important matters. Important Matter 2."

Benson paused for a second.

"We'll start in ten minutes."

* * * *

Bringing a baby into the Map Room of the Independent Transport Ship *Tulyar* wasn't strictly in line with Guild rules, as Kimmy Kumar O'Hanlon was not a member of the crew and could not legally be one until she was the age of 16. However, everyone ignored that rule as the freshly changed little girl was brought in and placed in a highchair by a corner of the 3D holographic table. On one wall, the blonde hair framed face of Security Officer Jessica Benson on the communication screen noticed the two of them come in, took a deep breath and began her briefing.

"Initial summary. Our cargo's been seized by New London Customs on the grounds of undeclared in the shipment."

"What?!" Captain Igor Lansky screamed, spittle flecking his thick white beard. Then he smiled wryly.

"Customs popped open one of the crates for a random inspection and found fifteen boxes of Lifter Prime. About nine thousand pills worth."

Sunita sniggered under her breath. Gunner David Maghreb looked confused.

"Sorry, what's Lifter Prime? Sunita – and why is it funny?"

"Sir," she said, "It's an aphrodisiac..."

"So, we've got our cargo seized because some sex pills were in it? We need to get that delivered within the next day or we're going to lose our shipping fee, which is like 200,000 gold marks..."

"270,000 credits in Terran money", Captain Lansky said, "That covers our entire operating costs for the next two months. Fuel, life support, wages. Then you've got whatever fine they want to levy against us for the fun tablets. Say 30 grand.”

“Oh, *jook rat.* So, we’re three hundred thousand in the red because of some pills in the cargo?” Sunita asked, “Who on Earth put those in there?”

Benson responded to this one, looking rather upset about this.

“Pyotr Randall. He’s under arrest now, pending a decision by the ‘Crown Prosecution Service’ on what to charge him with. With the permission of the Captain, I’ve fired him.”

“I assume you’ve told the First Officer.”

“I have. I can’t imagine she’ll disagree.”

First Officer Laila Rasheed was currently absent as she was recovering from a stroke.

“As I said earlier,” Lansky said, “If you’re going to engage in a side smuggling job, at least let us in on the action. Otherwise, you’re putting us all at risk.”

Sunita shook her head at this. Spacees had a general habit of dealing with their own problems and not drawing attention to themselves. Such as by breaking customs rules. While Sunita had herself spent time in a reform school for stealing a shuttle and been convicted of assault against a bigot, she tried to stay on the right side of the law unless morality trumped it. Serious criminal behaviour could and did get Spacers expelled from the community. Murder could get you airlocked.

"So, what do you want me to do about Randall's quarters?" she asked, "I assume he's not going to be coming back to get his items."

"Clear them out of course. Toss the clothes, mail him the photographs and keep the valuables."

* * * *

Having removed the last of Pyotr Randall's socks from his mess of a quarters, Sunita activated the cleaning robot, stepped outside and closed the door. Then she felt a hand on her left buttock.

"Hello, babe," she said, turning to face her husband and plant a kiss on his lips. She looked with approval at the red beard of Communications Officer Daniel O'Hanlon and hugged him. She felt a certain excitement and silently shook her head.

"Sorry, not now. Maybe later." she said, "I've still got to deal with this mess. Skipper then wants me to inventory the ship equipment and see if there is anything that we can sell for scrap value. Some of the space suits and welding equipment have probably had it..."

"I'll come and help you if you want. If you do get in the mood, then we've got somewhere nice and private..."

"Calm down, boy!" she playfully scolded him, "Anyway, who's got Kimmy?"

"Donna Faruk. Auntie Donna is trying to teach her Arabic."

"Arabic? The kid can't even speak Manglish yet! Anyway, I like Donna. Batty, but good batty. The Kawkab Al-Mushtari tribe are lucky to have her as one of their elders."

"Yeah, she's been called in as a judge in a property dispute down on the surface. Getting paid for her time as well."

"Which reminds me... we need to get some form of work. Once we've done all this, we need to get down to the surface and try to rustle some up. After the cluster that was this assignment, we're not going to be getting official work via the Exchanges, so it's down to chatting with people in even less salubrious bars again. I was never particularly great at the whole touting for business thing. Something to do with my attitude to old people with bad breath."

Daniel grinned.

"You've been getting my business for years and I've had no cause to complain..."

Sunita playfully slapped his arm.

"Calm down! Anyway, any of your lot in business down on New London? Who could do with some of their stuff being shipped off world?"

Daniel rubbed his beard.

"The Waterford Murphy clan run a good part of the farming business. The O'Hanlons aren't on the best of terms with them since the Great Maryland Punch-Up, but they might be welcome to pass some business to a Spacer. I'll come with you once I've done this."

"Got it."

Daniel started to turn away. Sunita looked at her husband's backside and decided that she needed some naked stress relief after all.

"Tell you what, I am up for some sex. I'll let you know when I'm finished here. Wear the red boxers, please."

* * * *

Six hours later, a less stressed Sunita Kumar pulled up to the entrance of Waterford Murphy Agricultural Produce in a hired all-terrain vehicle, turned off the engine and released the door locks for her husband to climb out. He walked over to the entrance gate and pressed the intercom as Sunita caught the distinct whiff of pig excrement that had been thankfully filtered out by the air filters during their journey.

She removed the key, opened the driver door and descended to the muddy ground below, hearing a slight squelch as her feet made contact. The rain had passed over, but it had clearly been heavy because of the large numbers of puddles in the vicinity. That and the river looked swollen.

She felt a dampness on one of her socks.

I need new boots.

She walked round to the gate, seeing three little pigs giving her a death glare.

"I'll have you with eggs," the big bad human said as a click and a loud buzz indicated the smaller side gate had been opened. Sunita instinctively reached behind her with the key fob to automatically close the doors and lock the vehicle, stepping through the gate as this happened.

The door to one of the barns opened and a dark-haired balding man with a barrel chest and blood-spattered overalls stepped out.

"Daniel O'Hanlon, as I live and breathe!" he exclaimed, "I'd give you a hug, but I've just delivered a calf. Six centuries of robot technology and we still have to deliver those things by hand!"

He looked at Sunita.

"This the wife?"

"This is *the wife, owl*" Sunita replied snidely, "Sunita Kumar. You are?"

"Declan Murphy. I'm in charge of the Bovine Division here. Five thousand head of cattle, all free range and producing some of the finest meat in the sector."

"Yes, about that meat," Daniel continued, "Who are you shipping it out with these days?"

"We're doing it through the Exchange."

"Come on, you're kidding. Who are you really getting to ship it out?"

"The *Exchange,*" Murphy emphasised, "We had several thousand litres of milk go missing last month and we were unable to get the insurance payment for our losses as there was no official record in it. So, the family had a vote on it, and we went for the Exchange. We've got a few tonnes of beef coming up next week, so you'll be able to grab it then."

Daniel sighed.

"We're in a *bitti* bind. Some idiot decided to do a bit of off-the-books smuggling in a legitimate shipment, got found out and the whole lot's been seized by Customs."

"Man, that stinks. What were you smuggling?"

"Lifter Prime."

Murphy burst into laughter.

"Would you guys be staying for dinner? The rest of the family would love to hear that story and maybe they can help you."

It was a very enjoyable meal, but there was no work available.

* * * *

At Dock 15 of Plaistow City, two of the shuttles of *Tulyar* were landed, conducting supply runs to and from the surface. As Sunita and Daniel arrived back at the dock entrance, they showed their Union of Irish Systems Starfarer's Passports to the security guard at the gate, then stepped inside where a young lady called Maria Penzance was holding a clipboard. Maria was the Officer Apprentice aboard *Tulyar* who was being trained in the ways of starship operation and being handed all the tasks that other people didn't want to do.

With her black leather jacket and thick brown bandolier (her pistol was stowed in the weapons locker), Maria may have looked like the 19-year-old that she was with a hair parting in the latest teen fashion, but you underestimated her at your peril. Sunita loved her in a way that she wasn't entirely sure was platonic.

She smiled at the two of them as they entered.

"Evening!" she said, "I've managed to get a rather interesting and potentially very lucrative opportunity. Although it's rather risky."

"Rather risky?" Sunita asked, "Can you explain please?"

"It involves doing work with a rebel group. Are you aware of the Bangla Freedom Front?"

"Yes…"

A couple of parsecs over was the Bangla Republic, whose once prosperous twenty systems were now under the control of a dictator by the name of Goran Marvin, whose Faith Militant ideology had taken over the largely Hindu system in a coup three years back, engaging in wholesale purges of his political opponents. Heavily sanctioned by most other governments, trade with the systems was limited and most people avoided the whole area unless they were desperate.

"Well, you know one of their leaders got sentenced to life imprisonment for those trumped-up child sex abuse charges?"

"Yes... Name of Orton Bradshaw. He oversaw the money laundering and fundraising for their group. They've lost a lot of cash as a result."

"Well, they think that they know where he's being kept and need someone to provide a fast ship for a jailbreak operation. They're willing to pay a million credits for it."

"A million credits? Are you sure that this isn't some form of trap?"

"This comes from a source that I trust."

"You have sources?"

"Well, she's... she's my aunt. She runs weapons to the rebels from time to time."

"How do you know she's not some form of trap?"

"Because... I just know, OK?"

Sunita shrugged. It was the best offer that they were likely to get around here.

"Get her down here and I'll get the Captain along. Benson as well."

* * * *

June Penzance was indeed Maria's paternal aunt, a curly-haired lady in her late 40s with a good number of wrinkles, several scars and a habit of chewing nicotine gum. As she sat inside *Pinnacle K14*, one of the four shuttles operated by *Tulyar*, she got straight to the point.

"Orton Bradshaw is located on Destitution."

"Destitution?" Sunita asked, "Sorry, what's Destitution? I know the systems around here very well and I've never heard of that one."

"Its formal designation is EL-361 or Saratoga. It's just inside Bangla space, but pretty far off the beaten track."

"Hang on, let me bring up a map."

Sunita turned around in her seat and brought up a digitised database of the human-explored galaxy. A quick search and she had found the system. It was only two parsecs from where they currently were; on the outer edge of the Hyades Cluster, it was a crowded neighbourhood. She read the description with increasing alarm.

Julie Benson beat her too it in the reaction.

"Hang on, they've got a penal colony on there? That's one of the most inhospitable life-bearing planets known to humanity. Carcinogenic spores in the atmosphere, venomous reptiles in the undergrowth, tree-dwelling creatures that will eat your eyes..."

"Why is it known as Destitution though?" Sunita asked.

"Someone tried to colonise it fifty years back. The costs, financial and human, involved in just keeping a research station there going bankrupted the operation and the facility was abandoned, with the system being marked as a 'Do Not Enter Without Permit' one. Bangla issues the permits." Penzance replied.

"Abandoned. Are you meaning to tell me that the Bangla Republic is using that as a penal colony?"

"Not so much a penal colony as a slow-motion death row. It's possible to live off the planet by hunter-gathering, it seems. For a certain time. Until something kills you. Drop your lifers there and it's a short sentence."

Sunita whistled.

"That's cruel and unusual punishment in any way you slice it", she said, "But why not just throw them out of an airlock?"

Penzance thought about this.

"Too many witnesses, even on a small ship. That or they don't want these people to have a quick death. Bangla still is officially a non-death penalty polity... and they could just claim that the planet killed them, so it wasn't murder."

Sunita raised an eyebrow.

"I doubt the United Systems Criminal Court would agree there."

"I don't know, I'm just speculating."

"Anyway, have you got any proof of this? Because if you got that out to the galaxy at large, there would be considerable awkwardness to Bangla."

"Bradshaw is the proof. We need to get him – and some others if we can find them – off the planet."

"Why do you need us?" Sunita asked.

"We need your ship. *Tulyar* is one of the Star Worker class, which is one of the fastest freighters out there. Both in hyper and with that powerful dampener system, your acceleration is quick. You're going to need that to get in and get out before the System Defence Frigate gets into range of you."

"Well," Lansky said, "It's not like we're going to be getting any other form of decent work round here and I hate those Bangla sons-of-rats anyway. I'll call a crew meeting in which you can outline your particular plan then take a vote."

* * * *

The mess room of *Tulyar* lacked a display screen. Or rather lacked a working one. As a result, Julie Penzance was forced to explain her plan involving a bucket, a collection of gambling chips and Kimmy's toy rabbit named Walter.

"Our source in the Bangla Navy tells us that a single *Ametist*-class frigate is assigned to guard Destitution, which is apparently one very boring duty indeed. There is no way that anyone on the planet can escape; the drop pods used to send them down do not have the fuel to reach space once they come down. They will take that ship out of orbit for anything half-way interesting.”

“We’ll need that ship out of orbit. *Ametists* are potent little beasts against any trader. While we have a two-barrelled cannon for self-defence, we have no missile capacity and no real way to stop one of their strike warheads,” Jessica Benson observed.

“Yes, 100 kilotons hitting you can ruin your day. So, we need to give them something halfway interesting. Fortunately, we have something nice and suitable.”

She grabbed Sunita’s coffee and tipped the contents out onto the table.

“Hey, *jell offa!*” Sunita cried out as espresso started to run onto her trousers.

“An Atomic Separation Munition.”

“Hang on, an ASM?” Benson said, “Of the sort used for large-scale mining operations? Do you have one of those?”

“Yes, we do...”

"You do know it's a Category A Felony to possess any atomic device without explicit authorisation from a recognised state. And I'm sure you're not up to date on your nuclear materials training."

"We're a rebel group, we don't care too much about laws. Also, we know what we're doing?"

"I really must protest. If we're discovered to be involved in an unlicensed ASM use, then we're looking at 20 years at least!"

"Do you have a better idea that gets these people away from orbit, Benson? As it's kind of your fault that we're in this situation in the first place?" Sunita said.

"How is it my fault?" Benson snapped, "I wasn't the one smuggling the sex pills in the first place. I can't be perfect all of the time!"

The Captain raised his hand.

"Have your fight later, ladies. Benson do you have another suggestion?"

"Yes..." Benson said, then stopped for a few seconds. Everyone turned to look at her.

"Well... it goes like this..."

She outlined the revised plan.

The vote was 15 to 3 in favour.

Chapter 3

Two days later, on board the *Ametist*-class frigate *Mumbai Six*, Senior Lieutenant Anya Mishal was two hours into another six-hour shift of utter boredom. There was only so much reading of technical manuals that you could do to keep yourself occupied on the long-range sensor monitoring job.

Nothing happened in orbit around Destitution. The system was far off any major trade routes, there was little of actual mineral wealth due to the lack of an asteroid belt and at any rate, the only slightly exaggerated stories about the wildlife on the planet kept people well away. Scientific permits were inevitably refused, much to the annoyance of scientists with a death wish, but still the secrets of what they were doing here were safe.

Her scope suddenly ended her boredom. She looked at the data reading and tapped a few buttons to bring the visual telescope round to examine it. On the screen, she could see the blue and white glow of a hyper pulse. Someone had jumped into the system.

She picked up the internal telephone.

"CIC, this is LRS. We have a hyper pulse bearing 020 by P29. Range unknown at this time."

Why haven't we been given monitoring satellites here?

"LRS, CIC received", came the reply, "Hyper pulse? Are your systems working properly?"

"LRS & CIC, this is Comms", someone else added, "We've got a rather strange text message just come through, timed sixty minutes ago. Seems some ship called the *Kentucky Fry* is here to do some mining operations and is going to be detonating a 'nuke' in three hours..."

* * * *

In the dense electrically charged dimension of hyperspace, the powerful drives of *Tulyar* were trying to push the ship into the inner realms of EL-361, so to speak. As you got closer to a large gravity source, hyperspace became thicker; something that also made entry and exit harder. Jumping into something as thick as concrete was not a good idea for any ship. Now they were flying through propane and they were going to need to get to the density of heavy water before they were close enough to the primary for a jump that would put them within easy reach of Destitution. Ship's Navigator Arlen Wilson was making the calculations for their location based on the other hyper beacons that he had a clear read on, something that was getting progressively harder as they pushed their way through. With hyper material, something you didn't want inside your ship if you valued breathing, starting to push them around, a certain drift was happening and needed to be compensated for.

Down in the starboard shuttle bay, Sunita Kumar was loading up a magazine for an assault rifle ahead of their mission down to the surface. A group of military surplus armoured Light Surface Warfare Suits with power assist were being tested by her husband (who would be staying behind) over in a corner to make sure that they were working. The suits were bulky and heavy, but they had protection against corrosive chemicals, atmospheric poisons and attacks by wild animals. Or lifers.

The latter were probably armed with spears, bows, slingshots etc. The suits could probably stand up to those, but Sunita wasn't keen on finding out, especially while wearing any equipment made by the lowest bidder.

A group of ten people had been put together for this assignment. Well, they only had ten armoured suits. Four hours after *Kentucky Fry* entered the system, *Tulyar* would exit hyperspace as close as it could get to Destitution. Rex Wolcott, the moustachioed maestro of piloting who was seen by most of the crew as a future captain of his own ship, would be handling the difficult job of pushing their way in, Wilson giving position cues.

Then two shuttles (*Pinnacle K14* and *Lavender G19*) would head down to the surface to the disused research station, find Bradshaw then take him off, along with any others willing to go that weren't pure psychopaths. Up to a maximum of sixteen as the shuttles could only take a total of 13 people each.

Pinnacle K14 had Megan Warner as its pilot, with Jack Williams as the operator of the auto cannon and backup pilot. Jessica and Sunita were joined with weapons loader Sunny Morris as the main 'manoeuvre group' for want of a better term. Although Sunita had suggested 'fire team'.

They would have about four hours to get down and get back up before the *Ametist* would be in range to engage *Tulyar*; if they were not back in time, the freighter would have to jump back out without them.

Which probably wasn't a good thing for those left behind.

* * * *

"This is your five-minute warning", the ship-wide address system rang out, "Ground crew to the shuttles. All other crew to their battle stations."

Sunita Kumar was already seated in *Pinnacle K14*, as comfortable as one could get in a large bright green armoured suit in a seat designed for a much lighter spacesuit or overalls. They'd had to make some adjustments to the straps ahead of the operation, so they'd be strapped in securely.

Benson was sitting in the seat next to her, looking over the last publicly available map of Destitution. They'd have to find the exact location of the research station on their initial approach.

At least they had an idea of roughly where it was supposed to be.

Finding Orton Bradshaw wasn't going to be too difficult. It was very unlikely that he was going to be anywhere else bar the vicinity of the former research station; it had the only decent shelter from the elements and wildlife on the planet, unless the Bangla government had installed another facility. Sunita doubted that.

There might be some form of automated defences on the planet's surface against attack. Penzance had ruled it out – they would have to be maintained and no-one was going to be sent down there unless they were a prisoner.

There were a lot of things that could go wrong here. But they needed the money and what was the worst that could happen? Death?

Sunita wouldn't mind dying, provided it was quick.

"Jumping out in ten, nine, eight..."

Sunita strapped herself in for the transition to normal space.

* * * *

With a bright blue flash and a slight lurch, *Tulyar* returned to the regular universe. In the front of the cockpit of *Pinnacle K14*, shuttle pilot Megan Warner looked at the spatial display on their screen.

Then swore rather loudly.

"The nav data's wrong! The nav data's wrong!" she cried out.

"What do you mean, the nav data is wrong?" Benson said.

"We're about a million kilometres further away from Destitution than we were supposed to be. Even allowing for margins of error in a jump, that's way over the distance we were supposed to be from the planet."

"That's not good", Sunita said, "We were supposed to have three hours on the planet to locate Bradshaw and get out... what are we down to now?"

It is entirely possible that Bangla has altered the orbital data to make this sort of thing harder to do... or it was just wrong in the first place. Oh, well.

"Two... we've got to fly there first..."

"Sorry, can't we use Tulyar's more powerful drives to get us closer?"

Megan paused for two seconds.

"Of course, we can... why didn't we think of that?"

"We can, but we've got another problem", Benson said, "Our pulse wasn't shielded by the planet, which means... that as soon as the light from it reaches the frigate, they will turn back and head straight for us."

Megan did some mental calculations.

"Hang on... 60 light minutes to the asteroid... I'll have to do some mathematics, but it will take them about four hours to get back... There shouldn't be a problem. We've got the same length of time..."

"But less searching time on the surface. Probably about two hours 45..."

"No *bori*, Dory", Sunita added, "We'll be fine."

* * * *

Fifteen minutes later, *Tulyar* had manoeuvred itself into a low orbit around Destitution, which would make the ship harder to see from a distance once the frigate approached.

A quick scan had determined the location of the research facility and a 120-minute orbit would put them over the region twice during time available.

The two shuttles would have to launch 30 minutes (give or take three minutes) before the second appearance to make the rendezvous.

A landing site was identified; a clearing about one kilometre from the entrance to the research facility. They would have to walk, but there was an access road that looked clear.

The shuttles undocked and began their descent into the atmosphere. Sunita checked the functioning of her weapon four times during the whole process.

"Are you detecting any transmissions from the surface?" she asked out of nerves, "Radar, radio, infrared, X-Ray?"

Warner shook her head.

"Sunita, this is a cargo shuttle. It doesn't have a passive scanning capability in anything bar computer-aided visual."

Sunita hadn't been that embarrassed since her trousers had slipped around her ankles when she'd proposed to her husband. He'd said 'yes' despite her boxer shorts.

They're comfortable. Don't knocker the boxer.

"Right. I knew that..." she replied, then tried to save the situation, "Any visual activity?"

"Well, there's what looks like a small hurricane moving in the nearby ocean. I'm not a weather witch, so I don't know which why it's going. Probably not a threat to us."

The two shuttles made a surprisingly graceful touchdown in the clearing, surrounded by thick foliage. The boarding ramp came down, Benson and Kumar stepping out first through the mosquito net curtains. While Benson was former Terran Union Special Forces and a positive gun dog, Kumar was a gun hamster at best. While she had seen combat as a ship gunner against two pirate ships, the only actual surface fight she'd been involved in was a mass brawl at her own wedding, started by a rival clan. She'd come out with a couple of bruises and to be honest, that fairy-tale carriage looked much better when it was on fire.

So, when a crude spear flew past her and bounced off the side of the hull, she instinctively fired 15 rounds of

10mm rifle ammunition in the direction it had come from.

* * * *

This ruined the day of a serial killer. As well as the rest of his life, because it is rather hard to function in any society with half a head and no right lung.

* * * *

There was a cry from the forest.

"Don't shoot! Don't shoot! I'm unarmed!" came a male voice, as a pyramid scheme manager in a tattered prison jumpsuit spattered with serial killer blood came out, his hands raised. This last statement proved to be untrue as he had a slingshot attached to a hook on his clothing where the chains usually went. He was also speaking Galactic Standard Manglish, as opposed to the Bangla Hindi more commonly spoken in the system.

Benson's face was visible through the clear armoured visor and Manager's face looked confused.

"You're not a Bangla Marine, are you? Marines don't wear bright red lip gloss and eyeliner. At least not in combat", he continued.

"Good observation skills. Anyone else with you?'
Benson growled.

"Just Luigi the Cannibal, but you shot him dead.
Praise to Lord Vishnu and Lord Ganesh for that."

Sunita looked confused at this. She'd just taken her
first life, something she'd not been keen on, but at least
she'd killed someone who wasn't going to be overly
missed. By anyone.

"What's your name and what are you in for?"

"Simon, Simon Saysan. I was... I..."

"Simon Saysan hurry up before I lose my temper."

"Fraud. Lots of fraud. About a million worth."

"Get in the shuttle. We're breaking you out, although
you may just end up in another prison. How do you feel
about testifying to the conditions here?"

"I want to say here... I'll die if I leave. You see, we're
all sick. There's an illness we all get. A virus that breaks
down your organs. You have to take a daily cocktail of
antivirals or you die."

Sunita raised her free hand in a stop gesture.

"You made millions by deceiving people and you fall for that old chestnut? They were using that in cults six centuries ago. One called Cygnus Alpha I believe. Get in the shuttle before you end up like Luigi."

"I... I... OK."

"Hang on", Benson said, "Have you seen Orton Bradshaw?"

* * * *

With four people staying to guard the shuttles, a party of six made their way down a dirt road towards the research facility. Well, it had been a dirt road once. Twelve years of lack of maintenance had resulted in road being replaced by a thick carpet of vines.

Some of which did not like being stepped on at all and had developed varying methods of expressing their displeasure. Like firing venomous darts or acid sprays in the direction of the person doing the stepping.

As Sunita walked past the remains of some form of mammal being consumed by associated carrion feeders with flies buzzing around all over the place, she was grateful that her filters were stopping the smell getting through. The air was breathable either way; it's just that with the filters removing the carcinogenic dust, her chance of getting some form of cancer was reduced considerably.

One quick turn around a corner and they were soon in sight of the crumbling remains of the Saratoga Scientific Research Facility and Colony. The formerly gleaming white buildings were well overgrown, with various windows having already been removed. There were some lights on the facility, which indicated that power was available, so someone was probably taking care of the nearby hydroelectric dam. A large satellite disc at the top of a hill had lost its transmitter and many of its panels.

"These colony transmitters are powerful enough to send a signal to a nearby system without the need for a hyper beacon." Benson said, bringing her Special Forces knowledge to commence the conversation.

"Why? It would take years for a light speed transmission to reach another system." Sunita observed.

"It means they can send off a final report when their colony dies."

* * * *

Back on *Tulyar*, Arlen Wilson was looking at the data on their scanners, looking for the *Ametist* frigate. It was too far out for radar to get a picture of its location, so that they were going to have to identify it from the vast gleaming cloud of space. This involved finding a moving object among all the non-moving ones. At 60 light minutes or so away, any ship was too far away to be seen visually via the optical telescopes used for finding position as well, so would have to identified by drive emissions (in the gamma ray part of the electromagnetic spectrum) or radio transmissions (on the other end of said spectrum).

This was very much an art as well as a science; many military frigates had emissions reduction systems to reduce their signature, although they would still stand out against the distant stars.

Tulyar, as a civilian vessel, did not have the capability to mask its emissions. Sure, the transponder was turned off, but the more powerful sensors would be able to make out *Tulyar*. The blue and yellow paint scheme of the vessel was quite distinctive.

A synthesised recording of an old-fashioned bell indicated that their passive scanners had found something. He moved over to the display and watched as the paper back-up system started to generate the results.

"Contact SO-13... grid location 418..." he said out loud, entirely unnecessary, "Apparent radio magnitude... Transponder pulse!"

The ship was squawking an ident! That meant that it wasn't too bothered about stealth...

"Transponder pulse reads B... H... W... A... R... 5... 9... 2..."

BH WAR... Bangla Warship. He fired up *Abby's Starships* and found the section on estimated emissions data of their *Ametist* class frigates. They had seven of the III Series, all purchased in 2609, just before the arms embargo...

He did some quick mental arithmetic against the apparent magnitude... and then, setting the ident as an Ametist III, got an estimate of the ship's current range...

"19 light minutes, give or take two..."

At a quarter of the speed of light, that ship could reach launch range in 72 minutes... And it was entirely probable that it had just seen their hyper pulse and soon as the telescopes were trained on it, they'd get a class ID at the very least. Give time to decelerate and turn around based on current speed...

"Oh, dear."

They had 100 minutes until they really, really had to leave.

Chapter 4

Entrance to the facility was through a set of solid metal gates that were firmly shut, next to a smaller gate that was currently partly open with a wooden barricade propped up against it.

As the party approached, someone fired an arrow that landed just short of Sunita's feet. Just before Sunita was about to end the life of a drug dealer, Jessica batted the weapon to one side.

"Let's not shoot everyone we meet, shall we?"

At this point, Sunny, who knew enough Bangla Hindi to get by, called out to the bow using drug dealer, who had clearly fired some form of warning shot only.

Sunita didn't speak a word of Hindi; she knew Tamil from her parents, but rarely used it in preference to Manglish and the limited Romany she used in Spacce circles. When she saw the barricade move back, she figured that whatever had been said had done the trick.

The drug dealer walked out towards them; arms open in exuberant joy as he sped towards his rescuers.

Then from stage right, something that resembled a tiger pounced on him. Jessica snapped off three quick shots, which succeeded in dispatching the creature, but it was too late for Drug Dealer, who had a large hole torn in his neck. Blood was spurting out of an artery and he was spasming rapidly as green venom entered his blood stream.

Jessica switched her fire selector to single shot and put Drug Dealer out of his misery.

"I can see why this planet got abandoned. The colonists must have been afraid to go outside."

She saw a cheery looking sign above the entrance welcoming them to the facility. She also realised that there was no way to fit through the gate in powered armour that was 2.3 metres in height.

"Guys, two of us are going to have to de-armour and go inside. One of those will be me... as for the other... ip, dip, doo..."

Sunita turned out to be 'you'.

* * * *

"'I love Toxic Waste'?" Jessica asked as she saw the T-shirt that Sunita was wearing under her body armour, which Sunny was now gathering to carry back to the shuttle. They were both wearing gas masks to avoid breathing in the air – a little of it probably wouldn't kill them, but it was best to take precautions.

"What?" Sunita said, "What's wrong with a comedy T-shirt?"

She was liberally applying insect repellent spray to her exposed skin to keep away the bugs here that could give your nasty diseases if they bit you.

"Not the sort of thing I'd been seen dead wearing. And to be honest, I really don't want you to be seen dead wearing it. It's two sizes too big for one thing."

"That's because it's not my T-shirt. It's my husband's. I'm wearing it for luck."

"How is wearing one of your husband's T-shirts supposed to have any impact on your survival chances?"

Sunny suddenly raised a hand.

"Guys, we've got a problem. We've been detected... we've got only an hour on this planet before we really must leave. That's so we can rendezvous with *Tulyar* and dock before they get clear of the planet's gravity well."

"No sense in hanging around here a second longer then", Jessica said, "We've already got one guy and he'll have to do.

"He's not Orton Bradshaw. He's a convicted liar and fraudster. No-one will believe his stories, and all of this will be for nothing." Sunita said.

"It already all is for nothing. We're not going to find Orton Bradshaw in the space of an hour and get him back to the shuttle in time for take-off."

"We don't need an hour. The pair of us are unencumbered by the suits and we can cover a kilometre in twenty minutes, if that, anyway. Thirty minutes to look round and see if we can find this guy or someone who hasn't run a Ponzi scheme."

"Twenty. And Sunny will cover the entrance in case any more of those man-eating tigers turn up."

"Yes, I don't think they share my taste in toxic waste."

* * * *

Sunita and Jessica walked through the now open gate, just as three murderers and a serial bank robber came out. Two of them were holding bows and arrows, one had a very nasty club and the fourth had a slingshot.

"A catapult?" Sunita said as the four came out, "What's that going to do?"

"Excuse me, my colleague has no appreciation of ancient weaponry," Jessica said, "That's a slingshot and I know it can be used to kill people if used correctly. Please don't kill her. Toxic waste needs friends."

"Who are you?" grunted the murderer with the nasty club and several missing teeth. "You don't dress like Bangla guards and they don't actually tend to come in here anyway."

"Well, I'm Jessica and this is..."

"Kidd. Billie Kidd." Sunita said. She was not going to give these people her real name, although she wasn't entirely sure where that name came from.

"What are you doing here? How did you get past the defences?" the murderer asked.

"We persuaded them there was some toxic waste they'd love. We're here for Orton Bradshaw."

"Bradshaw? I could have guessed someone would come for him. No-one is exactly going to come for Darius Khan, who killed his wife and her lover with a shotgun."

"Yes, where is he?"

"Asleep. We tend to sleep during the day except for a couple of hunting parties and a guard duty. It's too hot to do any heavy work while the sun is up. We'll take you to the mess hall. Don't mind the swinging corpse. We executed him for theft last week."

What Khan didn't tell her was the corpse smelt awful...

* * * *

The mess hall of the research facility was surprisingly clean, Sunita thought as they entered. Clearly there was some actual house pride here. She also noticed the large pile of metal tins and picked one up.

"Julie's All in One?" she asked. "You eat this stuff?"

She passed it to Jessica.

"This is dog food!" the security officer screamed.

"Humans can eat this, if they're desperate. Or drunk and playing Truth, Dare or Strip."

"Sunita, I don't want to know about your sex life, please."

"At least I have one."

Jessica was about to make some riposte to this when she saw a large white noticeboard. Half of it was covered in names and dates.

"That's our list of all those who have died here." Khan said.

"That's over 120 names! In two years!" Jessica said after a few seconds, clearly counting them.

"Out of 176 inmates dropped here. The longest surviving currently is a drug dealer named Sanjiv Mukhtar. He's on guard duty now. Or rather was."

"Sorry. His shift has ended permanently. Tiger."

"Shame. He was coming up to nine months."

"Nine months, *troo owli*?" Sunita said, "What kills you?"

"Wild animals when we go out to hunt, insect bites, sometimes heatstroke. Also, the very air can give you cancer and we have no facilities to detect it or treat it. Once people get too sick round here, we put them out of their misery."

"Or you execute them..."

Before he could respond, a dark-haired man with a long beard entered the room. He smiled with happiness.

"Are you here to rescue me?" he said.

"Yes, we are." Jessica said, "Now let's not waste time. We can't take everyone, and I really don't want to start a riot as you folks fight for the limited number of places here. Orton, Darius, let's go before the others figure out what is going on..."

She paused.

"How come no-one else heard the gunshots?" she continued

"The sleeping quarters are underground and soundproofed", Darius said, "Too many problems with late night animal noises. It would be our job to wake everyone up in an emergency."

"Let's not make it one."

* * * *

The five of them met up with Sunny and walked at a fast pace to the shuttle landing area.

"Hurry up!" Megan Warner called out from the ramp of *Pinnacle K14.* "Our launch window opens in one minute."

The group of them went into a jog to close the distance to the ramp. Orton Bradshaw was directed into *Lavender,* where Simon Saysan was already seated. It had been decided that Darius Khan would travel in *Pinnacle.*

As Sunita, bringing up the rear, got close to the ramp, she felt something wet under the foot... then tripped over. She turned to see what had happened and saw a group of sharp fangs dug into her right calf. Some plant was trying to eat her!

She felt something burning on her leg as Jessica ran back with her machete, cutting away a thick black root. Vile yellow and black liquid spurted out onto them, as the mouth of this vicious animal-plant cross clamped onto her leg. The limb of the plant was severed, and Jessica picked her up, taking her into the cargo compartment as Megan took her own seat to start up the shuttle's engines.

Lavender K19 rose up off the ground to their starboard side as Jessica grabbed a knife to start cut away the mouth, pulling away the teeth. Deep red wounds dripping with something white were visible, while her trousers were starting to smoke. Sunita suddenly felt her heart beating fast and herself starting to convulse.

She felt a needle going into her forearm, then everything went black.

* * * *

"What was that?" Megan yelled as she looked at the gore splattered Jessica.

"Shut up and take off! We need to get Sunita back to the ship!"

Megan did not need telling twice. She waited three more seconds to make sure that their companion was clear of the landing area and lifted off herself.

"Get her to a jump seat and strap in. I need to take us up to 2.5G for the orbit burn and I can't do that if you're standing!" she cried out.

She watched as the automated docking data came into the shuttle's computer system. This would get them into position to return to their ship and dock in the most efficient manner possible. Well maybe not the most efficient manner, but there was no time to be mucking about with anything fancy.

"We're strapped in!"

Megan pressed the buttons to initiate the automatic orbit sequence, activating her comms. There were seven people on this shuttle now – their first rescue had boarded the other shuttle. However, getting one of them back to the transport ship took priority over everyone else.

"*Tulyar*, this is *Pinnacle K14!*" she called out, "We have a medical emergency. Something venomous has tried to eat Quartermaster Kumar. We've administered a broad spectrum antivenom, but she's currently unconscious."

"Understood, *Pinnacle K14.* We'll have the med bay ready for you when you dock."

Megan watched as her heads-up display showed their increasing altitude... At 25 kilometres, the air-breathing engines would cut out and their chemical rocket engines would get them up to 100 kilometres where their main drive would take them into space proper. Below that, the main drive wouldn't work.

"Switching to chemical engines in ten, nine, eight..."

Red lights on a console generally mean that something is turned off or in a dangerous situation. When they turn up in an unplanned manner, there is a problem.

One turned up in an unplanned manner. She stopped counting.

O2 PUMP FAILURE

Don't panic. Don't panic. Switch to the back-up.

Then she realised. There was a major problem. The back-up pump could not be activated in the air. They would need to land to change over to the back-up.

"*Tulyar* from *Pinnacle K14*. We're unable to make orbit. The O2 pump we need to for the transition to edge of atmosphere isn't working", she said over the radio.

"*Pinnacle*, this is *Tulyar*. Stand by."

Megan looked back at Jessica, her de facto captain in this operation.

"I can get us back down and the pump swapped in fifteen minutes. The thing is, I'm not sure we have 15 minutes."

Jessica thought.

"Give me the mike."

Megan did so.

"*Tulyar*. This is Benson. We'll land, fix the pump and do what we can for Kumar. Jump and come back in twelve hours. If the *Ametist* is still there, jump back out and repeat."

"*Tulyar* copies. Good luck, *Pinnacle*".

* * * *

Tulyar fired its 100 gravity engines in a course heading away from the *Ametist* frigate. With their acceleration getting close to that of *Mumbai Six*, they'd have about three hours before the Bangla vessel could fire at them.

And we'll need those three hours.

Captain Lansky was standing in the Map Room looking at their projected course. With three hours at maximum safe acceleration, they would be running at over 9,500 kilometres a second and be about 50 million kilometres away. Not hugely fast in the grand scheme of things, but when translating into hyperspace, speed could be very important.

His Training Captain had described entering hyperspace when in an inner system to jumping into a swimming pool. Something that was OK when jumping off a diving board, but really a bad idea to do from the top of a ten-storey building.

Arlen Wilson had been pulling up their sensor records and calculating the relative density of the hyper material from their journey in system to work out where the safe point would be... it would be just before they were in nuke range and that depended on the hyper generator systems working first time.

Something that couldn't be guaranteed.

The door opened from the Bridge. Arlen was standing, holding a tablet on which he'd been making some calculations. He was standing in his normal smart stance, which considering the situation, demonstrated huge self-control.

"Captain", Arlen said, "I've got the calculations for you."

"Let's hear them."

"With the density records that I got from our approach, we will be able to jump safely in three hours time on our present course. In fact, we could probably jump safely five minutes before that. Ten minutes... it'll be a bit of a jolt."

* * * *

Lansky's only thing now was to wait. He made his way to his room and decided to try to sleep. With his Day

Room one door away and the Bridge only two, he was able to get there quickly in the event he was needed.

The gentle hum of the various systems of the ship working helped him go into a doze...

Suddenly, he woke. Something was off. Something was missing.

He got to his feet and reached for the communicator on his desk, making a voice call to the bridge.

"Bridge," he said, "Is something going on?"

The mature Scotch voice of the ship's chief pilot, Rex Wolcott, came in response.

"Aye, skipper", his tone was concerned, "We seem to have lost engine power. No change in speed for the last three minutes. Clarissa's down in the gubbins taking a look. She thinks it's a blown fuse. Will take her a couple of minutes to replace it."

Clarissa Müller, the ship's chief engineer, spent most of her time at the rear of the ship keeping an eye on the fission reactor that powered the main drives and most of the internal systems.

"Switch to using the reaction engines. That will give us five Gs of acceleration while she's fixing it. Keep them on once we're done."

"Is that wise, sir? We only have enough hydrogen fuel for an hour of that."

"If we don't get as much power as possible, we might be dead. Do it."

"Aye, sir."

Lansky heard the sound of the back-up rocket engines firing and realised they might be needed later.

"Belay that. Run it for half an hour and then stop. Tell Müller that if she can give us 105 once the system is back on, do so, but don't risk the compensator in doing it."

Lansky straightened his uniform. It was time to head back to the bridge.

* * * *

The fuse was quickly replaced, and the engineer got out of the crawl space before the engines ran up to 105. With *Tulyar* accelerating at 110 times the force of Earth's gravity, they were in fact keeping the same distance from their predator.

However, when Rex Wolcott cut the reaction engines as ordered and Müller put the nuclear drive back to 100 to avoid a dangerous overload, things started to get tight again.

* * * *

Lansky watched the map on his display. It was now very tight. A countdown on his own display showed the amounts of time before the Bangla frigate was in range and the point where they were able to jump based on Wilson's estimate.

There were 30 seconds between them; five minutes for the former and four minutes thirty for the latter. That was too tight an estimate considering they would have to cut engines for the hyper portal generation. That could take up to five minutes.

"Rex, activate the hyper generator now. That's an order." He felt the engine cut out and outside, he knew two beams of energy were streaking to a point ahead of them where they would combine to open a hole into hyperspace. A screen started to come down to shield them from the radiation and bright light of the pulse at this range.

"As soon as we get the portal open, Mr Wolcott, I need you to do a 180-degree horizontal turn and fire the engines at maximum power to soften our entry."

If we take serious damage in hyper, we might die in there... but we'll die if we stay out here for sure.

* * * *

Anya Mishal watched the chart as they closed towards missile range of the second intruder. They were two minutes away from maximum missile range and the ship ahead of them was just inside the nominal hyper limit now. They could already be firing up the jump portal generator.

Commander Dinesh Patel was sitting in his command chair, obviously thinking about how he was going to frame his report.

We messed up. We messed up big time. Unless we manage to destroy this ship...

"Sierra 2 has created a hyper pulse." The voice of one of their sensor operators confirmed the news that she'd been dreading. She turned her head and saw the bright flash that indicated their prey had opened a door into hyperspace.

"Sierra 2 has disappeared from scope."

The facility was discovered. Someone had gotten away with proof of a secret prison on a world as hostile as 'Destitution' and it was going to be an absolute embarrassment to their government. They'd managed to get a class ID on the ship before it had jumped, so that would make any enforcement action easier. There were not that many Star Workers out there, especially in blue and yellow.

They would now have to go down, recover all the surviving prisoners and take them into the regular penal...

"All crews, this is the Captain speaking", she heard Patel saying, "We are going to be activating Protocol Severin."

What's Protocol Severin?

Patel continued.

These men below are dangerous criminals and cannot be allowed to escape. Now that their location has been discovered, we must ensure that their criminal allies cannot return for them. Therefore, we will use a KT-16 missile to destroy the site."

What?

Anya got to her feet.

"Captain, I really must protest. This is an act in violation of interstellar law!" she yelled.

"Your protest is noted on the official record. This is a matter of necessity for the security of our people. We will fire as soon as we are in range."

He reached for a telephone.

"Security. I need a guard party up to the bridge to arrest Senior Lieutenant Mishal. The charge is insubordination and incitement to mutiny."

"You what?!"

"If she resists in any way, you are permitted to shoot her."

"Oh, for the love of..."

* * * *

Captain Lansky was sharply pushed into the back of his seat as the rear of *Tulyar* bore the brunt of the 'splash' into hyper. A couple of seconds later, the pressure disappeared and he started to rapidly look around. The lights had temporarily gone out... then came back on.

He called Engineering.

"Clarissa, how are we?"

The reply was a bit shaky.

"I'll give you a fuller readout shortly. I'm still alive, so is Joaquin. I think we're going to need a while to plug everything back in down here."

The captain terminated the call... and started to laugh.

* * * *

Sunita opened her eyes. She felt very, very wet and not in a good way; like she'd just come out of a swamp rather than a hot tub shared with a sexy guy.

She looked around and saw that there was still thick jungle visible out of the window.

"This doesn't look very much like *Tulyar*", she said, then felt some searing pain on her leg, "What the... Frinton... happened?"

She felt a slight stab in her arm and then looked down. Her trouser leg had been cut away and there was a thick dressing on her calf.

Jessica turned to her.

"You got bitten by a poisonous Venus flytrap thing with acid saliva and I saved you with the anti-venom. You're stable, but you really need to see a doctor. Then we had an engine failure and so we're lying doggo until *Tulyar* comes back..."

"How bad is my leg?"

"You're going to need a skin graft. I just gave you a painkiller."

"Great. That's another expense I can't afford. Mind you, I'll have to do it. My hubby's a leg man."

"I don't want to hear about your..."

Megan interrupted.

"There's something entering the atmosphere!"

Benson moved over to monitor the passive scanner screen.

"Single object, moving at 1.4 kilometres a second and... does that look like a ballistic arc to you?" she asked.

"Yes, that's not the way you'd take a shut... EVERYBODY, STRAP IN! WE'RE TAKING OFF NOW!"

Sunita was already strapped in. Her mind was already addled and the drugs entering her bloodstream were going to be making her more so. She tried to remember what things went in a ballistic arc as Megan started the take-off sequence.

"Er... what's going on?" she asked, "I'm on some good stuff and my cog nits san isn't very good..."

The shuttle was rising off the ground and starting to head away from the former research station at a maximum power climb. Sunita heard Jack Williams saying something...

Then everything went white.

Chapter 5

The 100-kiloton nuclear device detonated at the entrance to the main housing block of the research facility. The 500-metre fireball mercifully killed all those inside pretty much instantly. The facility disappeared in a flash.

Pinnacle K14 was struck by a thermal pulse that would have given anyone directly exposed to it third degree burns. The fact that the shuttle was shielded against this sort of thing stopped those sorts of injuries for everyone. However, the radiation protection was limited, especially when it came all at once.

The crew of the shuttle were exposed in one go to 500 millisieverts of radiation, the equivalent to 250 CT scans. This was half the yearly limit recommended for spacers.

This was currently not the biggest problem facing the crew of the shuttle, although it would be one that would emerge later. That was the blast wave that slammed into the shuttle a few seconds later.

It dislodged the main drive and rendered it useless. It broke two of the rear windows, rendering the vessel incapable of exiting the atmosphere. It also tipped it into a vertical spin, tipping end over end, heading towards a ridge in a ballistic arc that would drop it just over the other side.

Fortunately, Megan Warner was able to take appropriate steps to control it. However, by the time she managed to stop the roll and start the process of arresting the fall with the landing thrusters, she ran out of altitude.

Pinnacle K14 crashed into the trees nose first at 45 kilometres per hour.

* * * *

There was a slight sparking in the air as Sunita opened her eyes. The lights had gone out in the cabin after the impact... no, she had a face full of airbag. She brushed it away and lifted her neck up to an upright position. It hurt, as did a lot of things.

As her eyes started to adjust, she saw Jack Williams slumped in front of her... as well as a rather large tree branch that had punched through his armour and into his chest. The armour was designed to protect against small projectiles. Not huge ones.

Jessica moved in front of her and started to feel his pulse. She then swore.

"No, Jack, not you..." she said, then turned to the others, "Everybody sound off!"

Kumar took a few seconds to realise what she meant.

"Kumar", she said slightly weakly. This day had just gone from bad to worse. Not only were they stuck on an alien planet with lethal wildlife that had literally tried to eat her, they had just been hit by something and then crashed into something.

Six of them were alive and conscious, if all suffering from relatively minor post-crash injuries and a rather bad case of sunburn from the radiation. The shuttle had been sturdily built... except for the cockpit glass it seemed.

Megan Warner started to have a look at the computer systems, which had survived the crash.

"Warner, what's our situation?"

"We've crashed into a jungle canopy after a nuclear explosion hit us... I think we've been out for about five minutes or so. I don't honestly know. Also, we've got another problem."

"Let's hear it."

"We got whacked with a large quantity of radiation when the bomb went off. I think we're all going to suffer radiation sickness out of this, but a look at the overall dosage suggests we're probably going to survive. Around 500 millisieverts", Megan then remembered what had happened to one of the others, "Except for Jack..."

"Yes, we'll have to bury him somewhere. Or at least get him out of the way before he starts to stink."

"There's a third problem. We're transmitting a distress beacon and I can't turn it off."

"If the Bangla Marines come down, we can take them!" Sunita cried weakly.

"If they drop a nuke on us, I somehow doubt that."

"We can always try to shoot it down", Jessica said with a wry smile, "One last act of defiance..."

* * * *

As the giant electromagnetic event that was the result of their nuclear strike started to dissipate, Commander Dinesh Patel looked at what at the mushroom cloud that had emerged from the surface. With a 100-kiloton yield, the cloud was 'only' reaching about 12 kilometres into the air, so it would be easy enough to fly over to confirm destruction. They just had time for that.

They needed to get back to a habited system with a Hyper Beacon, where they could relay the situation back to High Command. He wasn't sure of the protocol there, just that he'd have to explain what had happened and it might cost him his commission.

His frigate could overtake *Kentucky Fry* and might be able to overtake the other ship, but there was no guarantee of that without a clear idea of where they were going. There were twelve possible destinations that they could go to within their jump range and none of them would welcome a Bangla frigate jumping into their system. Only eight would able to do anything about it, but still...

"Sir!" a rating cried, interrupting his thoughts, "We're receiving an automated distress signal from the planet's surface!"

Dinesh looked at the planet's display on his console, the location of the distress beacon marked on it. He made some quick mental calculations.

"We're jumping out", he ordered, "There's about an hour until local sunset, I'm not going to risk my people going down there at night and they're toast at any rate. We have to get to Lahore."

He paused.

"In case they do come back – or their comrades come back for them – leave the Rabid Sloth behind."

* * * *

Problem four had emerged a little later. The life support systems had packed up in the crash. They could open the vents and scrub the air of any contaminants, but there was a problem of the shuttle getting too hot. They had decided to lower the boarding ramp for proper ventilation and take the risk. Their cancer risk had already shot up a great deal as is.

"It's getting cooler", Megan said. They'd removed Jack's dog tags, taken the corpse and thrown it down a nearby slope. Spacers tended not to be overly reverent with the actual mortal remains, seeing them as garbage to be disposed after a quick ceremony. The dog tags would be the items brought along to the actual wake, where alcohol in large quantities would be consumed in his memory.

Jessica had started to hack away at some of the nearby plant life, trying to block off as many of the approaches as possible to the shuttle in the time they had left before the sun set.

Sunny was pulling out protein bars and bottled water from the ship's food locker. They were going to have to replenish lost fluids once everyone had gone through the first phase of radiation sickness, a not uncommon occurrence in this business. The fact they'd not thrown up within half an hour was a sign that the dose hadn't been lethal, but it wasn't exactly something you would do every day.

Sunita, still sitting in her seat, was watching all of this with increasing concern. With the injury to her leg, she wasn't going to be doing much walking any time soon. She had a weapon to hand, ready to make a heroic last stand. The bullets could penetrate light armoured suits of the sort they had, but she'd heard the Bangla Marines used a heavier type of armour. Jessica had advised them to aim for the head if possible.

The main lights had been turned off to make the shuttle harder to find in the dark and to improve their night vision. Only the red emergency lighting was on now as well as the external lights, so they had some view of the outside.

Out of the window, she could see an increasingly darkening jungle. Not that huge amounts of sunlight got down here in the first place even in normal conditions.

She was starting to feel increasingly warm and nauseous. At some point, the group of them were going to hurl, probably in quick succession. It was time for one of her patented bad jokes.

"What's yellow, black, dead and flies?" she asked those present in the shuttle.

"I don't know…" Megan said, "But I get the feeling you're going to tell us."

"A zom-bee!"

Megan groaned.

"Really, that's awful. How does your husband react to those jokes?"

"Well..." Sunita did not finish her sentence before she gagged once, gagged twice... and projectile vomited onto Megan's back.

Fortunately, that was the only time someone vomited *in* the shuttle.

* * * *

Three hours passed. The sun had completely gone below the horizon now and the six survivors were all inside, trying to conserve their energy after the bout of sickness that had mostly passed.

Then Jessica, who was on watch by the ramp, raised her hand. She was wearing night vision goggles usually used by Megan for a night landing.

"I hear something."

She got to her feet, moving towards the ramp. She leaned forward to stick her head out of the door to see what the noise was. If someone had come down to the surface and was armed with a sniper rifle, there was a decent chance her blonde brain would be spread all over the cargo bay.

She would have to be quick. Two seconds at best.

Three, two, one.

She stuck her head out and saw something about 25 metres away. It looked like... a large koala? A koala standing on its hind legs... and carrying a spear?

She ducked her head back.

She turned toward the others.

"Do you remember if the reports on this planet mentioned drop bears?"

Megan turned towards her and started scratching her head.

"Not that I recall... but those creatures are very good at hiding."

Then she pulled out a small clump of hair.

"We've encountered them on sixteen planets so far. Guess that's seventeen."

'Drop bears' or *Phascolarctos sapiens stillabuntus*, were an alien species that had turned up in colonies on various worlds, usually killing livestock but occasionally terminating humans. The 'drop bears' would often wait in the branches of trees, then drop on the head of the prey before cutting its throat with razor-sharp claws. Some of them had been seen using spears... or even stolen pistols.

Jessica raised the rifle and took aim at the creature.

"Bye bye Cushelle..." she said, but before she could finish the one liner, the bear saw her and tossed a spear in her direction. Jessica instinctively ducked out of the way, but the spear fell well short.

She moved back... and it was gone.

"Well, good riddance," she concluded and sat down on one of the seats in the cargo bay, closing her eyes, rubbing her head... and pulling away a clump of hair.

"Oh, *baro*. I'm going to need a wig."

* * * *

90 minutes passed with nothing more exciting than a venomous snake that Jessica shot before it got close. Then they heard something weird...

It was like a grunting choir. As in a group of singers all grunting to a tune instead of, well, singing. Jessica got to her feet and raised her rifle.

Entering the clearing that they'd created by their crash landing was a large mass of fur, wood and sharpened flint about fifty metres away. They moved towards the shuttle ramp, starting to spread out into a square. They were waving their spears up and down, vocalising like crazy.

"Guys!" Jessica yelled, "To arms! We're about to be charged by Ewoks!"

The others had already got to their feet and now moved towards the cargo bay, readying their assault rifles to fire at the creatures who clearly wanted to kill them. Except for Sunita, who was still not able to stand on her injured leg. The seats were unable to rotate, so she was facing completely the wrong way, but she could just turn about turn around. Jessica had just given her a pistol when the grunting stopped... and was replaced by a full battle cry.

About sixty – none of the humans were counting at this point – drop bears charged towards them.

"Fire!" Jessica screamed, but she didn't need to say this. Five rifles spat hot death from their barrels as 150 rounds of full metal jacket ammunition sped towards the shuttle. Cuddly murder teddies fell left and right, but not all the bullets hit home. With about a dozen still running towards them, Jessica at that point realised that there was a better option. She punched the button to lift the ramp...

Two drop bears managed to jump onto the ramp as it was raising. One of them was shot by Megan as she was reloading and fell to the ground. The second leapt for Jessica's chest. Then its head exploded, showering her with little bear brains.

She turned to look behind her. Sunita was holding a smoking pistol.

"Good shot!" Jessica cried out and started to wipe offal from her face. "Yuck, I hope these haven't got chlamydia."

"Well, that's the only way you're ever likely to get it." Sunita quipped.

"Ha ha. Now what are we going to do about the demons outside?"

The ramp was fully closed now, and ten angry drop bears were standing outside, screaming and banging against the door.

"You could sing to them... they'd soon go away."

Jessica gave Sunita the finger.

* * * *

"Ready to exit hyper in ten seconds."

Captain Lansky moved to strap himself into the jump seat in his day room. It had been a very worrying 12 hours since his ship had exited the system and popped out to just beyond the system's heliosphere, beyond the detection range of the frigate. He had tried to get some sleep during that time but got an hour at best.

Five of his people and one of the prisoners were missing in the system. He had no idea of what had happened to them. The other guys they'd rescued had been put on *Kentucky Fry,* which was heading to New London. Penzance had told him that he was going to get the full million and he had no obligation to go back for anyone.

He had told her very firmly that he was not abandoning his crew unless he was sure they were dead.

Sunita Kumar had joined his ship three years earlier, as part of a package deal with her husband. He'd made her Quartermaster based on the recommendation of her Training Captain who felt she had a good career ahead of her despite having to fire her for assaulting a passenger who had been abusive to an alien colleague. She was witty and quick with it, which he liked, but most importantly, she was very organised with a strong recall of stock levels.

Jessica was a very smart security chief. A bit cold and stern, but you didn't want a raving drunk in charge of your security. Megan was a great shuttle pilot. Sunny Morris was a strong and efficient weapons loader. Jack Williams was a pretty good shot as well.

He really did not want to have to write letters to their next of kin.

There was the sharp lurch as they returned to normal space. It was now a case of establishing their position, seeing if anyone else was there and making the appropriate plans.

He reached for the concealed carton of whiskey and poured himself two fingers of brown liquor. Two minutes later, the intercom rang.

"Captain, it's O'Hanlon. We've got good news and bad news."

"Bad news first."

"*Pinnacle K14* is broadcasting an automated distress signal from the surface of Destitution. We're plotting a fast time course to get us into orbit. That leads us to the good news."

Lansky was processing the bad news at this point.

"There's good news?"

"The frigate appears to have left. It's certainly nowhere near the planet. We have time to get down to the surface and confirm what is going on."

"Or send them a message first."

* * * *

After four further hours, the drop bears had given up and let them be. At this point, the shuttle was starting to get rather stuffy, so Jessica decided to crack open the ramp a little to let some air in. It was starting to get light outside; the sun was clearly above the horizon, but not yet shining through the trees.

The others were sitting down, mostly asleep. Megan was awake, looking out of the front window. Then came two excellent chimes.

"Everyone! Wake up! We've got an incoming message! It says 'Pinnacle, are you there?' *Tulyar* has come back!"

"Has it been that long? They actually came back?" Sunita said as she woke.

"Sunita, you've been a Spacee for how long now? 23 years?" Megan asked. "Surely you should know that you generally keep your word." As she said this, she was typing a message back to the ship informing them of the situation. Everyone was quiet as they waited for the reply from *Tulyar* to come back; what with the light speed delay.

Sunita tried to ease the tension.

"A drum kit fell off a cliff. Ba-doom-tish."

Jessica groaned.

"Why did your husband marry you? It clearly wasn't for your jokes."

"It was actually. And many other skills I have".

Then the reply came through Megan read it.

"They're about ninety minutes out. The System Defence Frigate has left the system, so we're free and clear now. Soon we'll be out of here."

It soon became clear that 'soon' was a relative term.

* * * *

"The nearest clearing that the other shuttle can fit in is four kilometres away. That's a good hour's walk in normal conditions, but this isn't normal", Jessica briefed the crew, "For a start, Miss Kumar here..."

"Mrs Kumar", Sunita corrected her.

"Mrs Kumar is incapable of walking without assistance. We're going to have to carry her on a stretcher, which is also going to slow us down. Also, with those drop bears out there, I want to have us in as big a formation as possible. So, we're going to wait for the other party to come down to us. They're five strong and with six of us here, there's two people short of a powered armour suit. They'll be able to bring another two over for us and then we can return to the ship as one group."

"I can't put an armoured suit on", Sunita said, "Certainly not without assistance."

"We'll do what we can. After Drop Bear O'clock, I'm not taking any chances."

Ninety minutes later, there was a sharp volley of automatic fire that made everyone jump.

Megan hit the communicator.

"*Lavender,* what was that?!"

The voice of Daniel O'Hanlon came back over the radio.

"There was some psycho teddy bear thing outside the ramp. Which none of you told us about!"

"Yes, sorry about that. We've not had a great day." The sheepishness in Megan's voice was obvious even to Sunita in her not 100% 'with it' state.

"Is there anything else that we need to know about? Like pink elephants?"

* * * *

Sunita watched as the ramp lowered to reveal the rescue party, including Daniel. She felt her heart beat a bit faster and mentally reproached herself.

I can do the sex later.

"Hi, honey. Sorry for my appearance." She said with a smile.

"You still look fine to me, babe." Daniel replied, and Jessica raised her hand.

"Snog later," Benson said, "We need to get out of here."

"Yes, about that..."

"Explain!"

"The path to the shuttle landing site runs along a cliff edge and the rocks above look a bit iffy. We'll have to be very careful and make sure that we don't make any sudden loud noises."

* * * *

Sunita was looking up as Daniel and Jessica carried her stretcher along the clifftop path. This was a good thing as she didn't have a sight of what was a rather long way down.

The radiation sickness was starting to come back again – the rescue team had brought over some pills to help with the effects of the radiation dose, but she was still feeling nauseous. They'd have to be checked out more thoroughly back on the ship to make sure how bad the radiation dosage was.

Not sure how much of an expert Megan is on radiation poisoning. I hope I don't die. That would stink for Kimmy and Daniel. Well, it would stink for me. Heaven might be nice though...

They were walking below a group of very loose rocks. Sunita's vision was a bit flurry but she saw something furry moving about them. Her injury addled mind processed something and then she tried to say something.

"Drooo... Drooo..."

Jessica looked down at her from the feet end of the stretcher.

"Just relax, we'll be back at the ship soon..."

"Drop... drop bear!"

Jessica quickly lowered the end of the stretcher and unslung her weapon, just as a series of large rocks started to roll down the cliff towards them. Things seemed to go into slow motion as the big objects descended. She saw Jessica firing up in the direction of the rocks, then watched one tumble straight into Darius. Half his height and weighing several hundred kilograms, it swiftly carried him off the cliff path. A long scream could be heard before it suddenly stopped.

Jessica was looking down at something, her mouth wide open. She ran a hand over her sweaty brow.

"Double time, everyone! Go as quickly as you can before any more of this lot show up!"

They got to the new landing site without any further incident, but the mood among everyone was now distinctly subdued. They'd retrieved three prisoners from the planet. They now had two.

The ramp was opened and Sunita's stretcher was placed on the cargo bay, securely strapped into place. Everyone else took their seats as Rex Wolcott started the take-off procedure.

She was looking up at the ceiling of the shuttle; the only thing that she was going to see during this whole flight. Her head was throbbing from the radiation sickness currently working its way during their system.

"Good news is that what fallout there was appears to have gone pretty much all in the other direction..." she didn't recognise the voices in her state.

"We'll need to make sure there's no traces on the shuttle when we get back to *Tulyar.*"

"No point in doing it here. We might run into some fallout in the atmosphere."

"OK, initiating launch sequence in... Is that a drop bear, by Jupiter?"

Five rapid fire cracks. Then Sunita heard the ramp close.

"I've had *enough* of drop bears for one lifetime. The Gan evolved from those?"

"Not directly..."

The slight increase of gravity as they took off, then a slight shudder. A few seconds of rising, a slight tilt, then the climb began.

A string of flight information, that she wasn't paying much attention to. She was in an increasingly delirious state.

"SAM, three o'clock low!"

A sharp lurch to the right and a steep climb, followed by a sharp dive. Then everything went black.

Chapter 6

"Sunita... Sunita... Sunny... wake up, *mort...*"

She felt something cold on her face, trickling down her nose and into her mouth. She opened her eyes, to see the face of her husband.

"Was that really necessary?" she groaned. Pouring a bottle of water onto her when she was sleeping was one of her husband's favourite pranks.

"Well, it woke you up..." he said and kissed her on the forehead. Sunita tried to get to a seated position and then realised that she was still strapped to the gurney.

"Where are we?"

"In orbit on a rendezvous course with *Tulyar.*"

"So... we're not dead. Where did the SAM come from?"

"An automated defence battery left over from the days of the research station. I'm not an expert in radar systems, but it appears that the missile guidance had broken down or something. That's what Megan said. I'm just grateful that we're alive."

"We need to get out of here fir…"

She started to gag. Fortunately, Daniel tilted the stretcher, so she could vomit on the floor.

* * * *

The shuttle docked and the group of them were faced with the stern matriarch that was Doctor Alison Donovan, who had survived two husbands. Some said that her stare had killed them.

At any rate, she was dressed in a hazmat suit.

"I'm going to need all of you to go through the decontamination suite. Remove all your clothes, place them in the incinerator chute and then give yourself a through scrub down in the showers."

Sunita, now in a wheelchair that had been brought with them, raised her hand.

"Er, Doc?" she said, "I don't stand up on my leg. How am I going to wash myself properly?"

She could feel her husband's hand tighten on her shoulder behind her.

"I'll come in and wash you myself", Doctor Donovan said.

Her husband let go.

"The last time you two were alone in a decontamination shower", the doctor continued, "you produced something that has since vomited all over one of my nicer blouses. I'm going to make sure I scrub you very thoroughly – and you're not going to enjoy it."

Sunita gave her two fingers in advance... then vomited over her trousers.

* * * *

Back on the bridge, Captain Lansky was double checking their route out of the system. You wanted where possible to enter hyper going in roughly the same direction as your destination, to save on having to make a complex navigational turn with no visible stars to guide you.

"I make our burn point four minutes away", he said, "Do you agree, Rex?"

"Yes, sir", Rex replied, "I most certainly do. Just a case of..."

"New contact, bearing 240 by Papa Zero One!" Arlen yelled, "Rapidly accelerating on a collision course!"

"Rex, make the burn now!" Lansky said as he moved to send an all-ship announcement, "All hands, brace for emergency maximum thrust!"

His repeater showed the object heading towards them. The numbers next to them rapidly started to increase. He saw their projected courses crossing each other...

"Raise nose 15 degrees!"

"Aye, sir!" Rex pulled back his steering column. Out of the window, Lansky could see a white object streaking towards them... then rapidly moving past.

The figures on the screen indicated that it was slowing down, arguably getting ready for another pass.

"Arlen, what do you think that is?"

Wilson turned from his own console...

"I... I..." Wilson stuttered. Lansky remembered that Wilson had never seen any form of physical combat before today, at least involving spaceships. First time panic could be forgiven.

"Rabid Sloth!" Rex yelled, "Powered down nuclear attack drone. They wait in orbit for a while and then attack a target. They're banned like all fully autonomous weapons systems."

"Well, the Bangla nuked a prison camp from orbit, so I doubt they care about the Seventh Geneva Conventions..."

"If there's a nuke on that and it gets close, we're smoked mackerel."

"And deep frozen to boot."

Wilson called out again.

"It's stopped... and starting to come back..."

Lansky looked at the numbers... and smiled.

"Wilson, look at the velocity figures and an acceleration calculation."

Lansky was positively grinning now.

"Speed Factor 98 for the drone... and Speed Factor 103 for us. We're pulling away."

"We most certainly are. Wolcott, pull us back to 100 acceleration. Wilson, keep an eye on the drone. If things stay the same, we should be fine."

Things did in fact stay the same... and they jumped out of the system four hours later.

They were, however, not going to be fine.

Chapter 7

Two days passed. The hyper journey was complete, the shuttles were sent down to the surface with the rescued prisoners.

Sunita was lying on her bed, watching her daughter whacking away at the side of her cot with a rattle and making happy noises. They were starting to introduce Kimmy to more solid foods now, but she was still going to need breast milk for a while. Speaking of breast milk...

She'd been advised that it would not be safe to feed Kimmy naturally for a week until the radiation had fully left her body, but in the meantime, she was going to need to 'pump and dump'.

She reached for her intercom to call her husband. She was in addition to the radiation issues, still recovering from her encounter with a venomous plant and her leg was too weak to do much walking. Even to get the breast pump on the other side of the room was challenging.

"Daniel, can you get Pump Bravo for Important Matter Three, please?" she asked. Two minutes later, someone entered the room.

"Daniel, I wasn't expecting you to shave, dye your hair blonde and turn into a woman".

It was Jessica Benson, who walked over and passed the breast pump over to the Quartermaster. As Sunita made her own expression, Jessica sighed.

"We've had a bit of a problem with the New London authorities. Specifically, with Orton Bradshaw."

"What do you mean?" Sunita asked.

"Bangla filed an arrest warrant with the authorities for him."

"They're never going to hand him back over to the..."

"I haven't finished, Kumar. They sent over a load of evidence from their embassy to the Ministry of Justice. The New London CPS is looking at it in full, but at present, she's refusing to grant him admission to the planet's surface. He's stuck in immigration."

"That's a problem. I'd never put New London in that camp, but..."

Benson sighed again.

"They sent over three reams of evidence and associated data discs. Witness testimonies, copies of the seized child pornography, forensic evidence."

"It'll be faked."

"I thought so too, but they don't think so. We're getting a lawyer to look, but I've got a nasty feeling that Bradshaw is guilty as charged on at least some of the counts against him. I'm no forensic expert, but some of this stuff is very hard to fake. Especially in this much detail."

"*Ā arumai.* The fact that they had this ready to go suggests..."

"They were expecting an escape. The System Defence Frigate must have sent a message as soon as it reached the Lingyuan system. That's less than a parsec. Half a day for a ship like that. Hyper message to Goa-Kerala then relayed to New London. They beat us here."

"There must be a leak on Julie Penzance's end. I've told her. She'll let me know what she finds."

"What's your suggestion?"

"See what the lawyer says, then put Orton under a polygraph."

Benson stopped suddenly, reaching into her pocket to look at her comm. She swore violently.

"That doesn't sound good. Doesn't sound good at all."

"No, it's not. Not at all."

* * * *

Captain Lansky looked at the unconscious form of Simon Saysan, as the doctor took a blood sample from the master of *Tulyar*'s arm. He didn't feel it as he processed the shock. Saysan had been looking slightly unwell as they were coming down from the ship, but he'd chalked that down to the change of atmosphere.

He had been in discussion with Captain Stanton of New London Immigration about Orton Bradshaw when there had been a commotion from outside. The two of them left the office to see Simon on the ground, starting to bleed from every orifice. Everyone had been rushed into quarantine.

Saysan was now in a coma and it wasn't looking good. The sample had been rushed for analysis at the pathological lab, but anything that caused that sort of bleeding with little notice was clearly dangerous.

He was sitting on the bed, hoping that he hadn't got whatever Simon had come down with. He hadn't thought to request an infectious diseases blood test on the people that were coming from the planet. Neither had Doctor Donovan, who had been looking for radiation sickness. Now he thought about it, she had been getting more forgetful in recent months.

All in there, they had just committed a major procedural omission that had put his entire crew in jeopardy. Not to mention an entire planet.

Tulyar would now have to be impounded, the ship thoroughly checked over for any signs of whatever this was.

"Doctor?" he said.

The doctor turned to him.

"I need to use a communicator device", Captain Lansky asked.

"Why, may I ask?"

"I need to report myself to the Spacer's Guild. For possible criminal negligence."

* * * *

The Quarantine Team arrived on *Tulyar* shortly afterwards. Wearing hazmat suits, they were as friendly as they could be for these sorts of people. Sunita and Benson all had to give blood and saliva samples.

Benson wasn't feeling ill, but you never knew with these viruses. She made sure that her will was updated just in case.

Twelve hours later, the Captain gave her a call. She took it in her quarters, standing to attention as she braced herself for the news. He didn't look very happy.

"Benson, the laboratory on New London has identified the virus. It's something called Kongzhi-C. It's a biological weapon from the 21ˢᵗ century, developed by the former People's Republic of China."

Benson ran through her history lessons for the 21ˢᵗ century. The collapse of the US, the Chinese Century, the African Rising, Ava Rice's initiation of a nuclear war in 2099...

"Basically, it was a sort of rapid effect Ebola-style virus used against political dissidents. Anyone injected with it would require special medicine, something called antivirals, on a near daily basis for the rest of their life. Good news, it isn't contagious unless you're exchanging blood or semen... bad news is that both Simon Saysan and Orton Bradshaw are infected with it. Worst news is that the electronic records on any antivirals would have to be requested from Earth and transmitted via Hyper Beacon... or obtained from Bangla. Either way, we're likely not going to get anything synthesised in time before they both die."

"So, can we do anything?"

"Pain management only. They're not going to put them out of their misery just in case we can get a cure over."

Benson's face was a mask. There was a long-standing practice among Spacees of administering a coup de grace to mortally wounded comrades and many had standing instructions for this to be done rather than let them suffer. Decompression injuries were very nasty.

"I'd like to come down and confront Bradshaw with the evidence of his illegal activity before any decision on pain management is made, sir."

"Why?"

"He's a paedophile. I want him to suffer in his final hours."

* * * *

Jessica Benson was standing in the airlock for the quarantine area, adjusting the face mask as the scanner ran from the floor to the ceiling to detect any toxins in the air. It probably wouldn't be a good idea to break wind right now.

As the inner door popped open, she heard the urgent sounds of a crash alarm. Medics rushed into one of the rooms as she quickly followed. They soon crowded around the figure, but a quick read of the name on the door told her everything. S. Saysan.

Five minutes later, as life was pronounced extinct, the number of people who could bear witness to conditions on Destitution had been reduced to precisely one.

And that one is fatally compromised in more ways than one.

* * * *

A hundred credit bribe was enough to buy her ten minutes of time with Orton Bradshaw. She entered the room, a touchpad in her hand on standby mode. She saw Orton lying in the bed, hooked up to a series of monitors. It appeared that the virus hadn't yet reached the number of copies in his bloodstream to start having a deadly effect; it likely wouldn't be long.

"Good morning, Jessie!" Orton cried out as she entered. He was looking surprisingly chipper.

Had he been told that he was going to die?

"My name is Ms. Benson", she said, as she placed the tablet on the table next to his best and woke it up to display one of the less disgusting images that they had received, "Please explain this."

He looked at it and a small smile appeared for a fraction of a second before he turned away in apparent disgust.

"I have no idea what that is. Put it away."

A security officer had to be pretty good at reading body language and Orton's reaction... was off.

"I don't believe you. This was found on your desktop. Along with four hundred other images."

"Not mine."

"Your banking records suggest otherwise."

"My bank account was hacked."

"Funny how you didn't report that at the time."

He swore at her.

"You're doing their work! Discrediting me discredits my movement. Do you want a free Bangla or not?"

"Of course. But I can't let someone as clearly evil as you near the levers of power."

"Doesn't matter. I'll be dead soon. Our ideals will live on."

"Perhaps, but I'm going to advise that the movement quietly erase you from history. If they win, you will have played no part in their victory."

He swore again.

"Also, I'm going to inform the doctors about your crimes. I think they're going to make some mistakes in the pain management."

She started to walk out the door, then stopped.

"Don't worry, you'll have clarity of mind to think about what you've done and get ready to meet your maker."

With that, she went to the bathroom, locked herself in a cubicle and cried.

* * * *

Benson exited the quarantine area, where she was met by Maria Penzance, holding a large sports bag. The young woman was looking like she really didn't want to hold the case.

"I've got the money for the operation", she said, "A million credits in 50 credit bills. It weighs something like 20 kilogrammes."

"Could they not have given it in a more manageable format? Like currency plaque?"

"Not without it being traceable back to them. This whole operation has turned into a bit of a farce; they have no real evidence that Destitution ever existed as a prison."

"Er... Tulyar took some orbit photos."

"Of an abandoned science facility."

"So, we lost a crew member for nothing."

"Not nothing, a million credits."

"We might not have that after bringing a deadly virus to this planet... Fines for biosecurity breaches can be steep. Even the million we got wouldn't cover that. Suppose you could say that Destitution has to led to destitution of our own."

* * * *

Sunita was trying on her new wig when they came. Sitting in the Quartermaster's Office, looking at the mirror, the internal public address system went off, with an unfamiliar voice.

"This is Commander Abigail Stetson of the Royal New London Defence Force. Your ship is being seized by the New London government for involvement in criminal activity."

Sunita looked up and started to look towards the gate that separated the weapons area from the rest of the stores. She had one of the keys to it.

Criminal activity? Well, with smuggling charges and biosecurity breaches in two separate visits...

"Do not attempt to depart the system. Do not attempt to destroy or dispose of any equipment. Failure to comply with these instructions is a criminal offence."

New London can hack our internal PA system. What else can they hack?

"We will be boarding this vessel in ten minutes. Prepare to be searched. Resistance will be met with deadly force."

They could run, sure. But no system in established space would touch them. Heading out into the ungoverned systems was possible, but how long could you survive out there?

Spacees run from unfair justice. But not from fair justice. This is fair justice.

Then Lansky's voice came over the PA.

"All crew are to comply with New London's instructions. That is an order."

There was a pause.

"My apologies. I started that wrong. The ship is being forfeited as payment for the biosecurity breach, which Doctor Donovan and myself will take full responsibility for. This is a great ship and it has been agreed that the ship will be commissioned into the New London Merchant Marine as Fast Transport Ship *Tulyar.*"

Oh, no. Oh, no. Spacees are not government suits. We assist when requested and suitably compensated, but we wouldn't do it full time.

"All crew have the option to stay or leave as they see fit. I will give you references for joining a new crew. Those who wish to remain with this crew are to report to the bridge tomorrow at 0900 where the new Captain will be waiting. One at a time, please."

There was a cry from the cot. She turned and saw her daughter was making a cry that she guessed was a request for feeding. She was starting to be able to tell them apart; although it was probably just as much Kimmy being able to make different noises for different needs.

If it was me, I would be walking off this ship. If it was just me and Daniel, the same. But now there's three of us...

* * * *

Sitting in the Captain's Chair, Vanessa Widomski, new Captain of FTS *Tulyar*, surveyed the bridge of her new command. She was debating whether to keep her reading glasses on or off for this session; this would be her first meeting with whoever wished to join the new crew and she wanted to make the right impression. When you were an attractive human in your early 40s, you needed to find a way to be taken seriously and seen as competent rather than just 'set dressing', a sadly common practice. A

~ 117 ~

pet tarantula on your desk tended to help, but she'd died last week.

She put her glasses on as the sliding door opened and a medium height Asian woman with mid-length dark hair entered, dressed in the dark blue jumpsuit that had been the uniform of *Tulyar* to this point. Vanessa was herself wearing the brown uniform of the New London Merchant Navy.

The woman entered the room and gave the slight look of confusion, with the teeniest of smiles.

"Are you the Captain or has he hired an escort?" Sunita Kumar quipped as she entered and moved to a neutral spot in the floor where she snapped to attention. Not very well.

"If you're going to last long around here", she said, "I would strongly advise you to not make crude jokes to the face of your commanding officer."

She saw Sunita visibly gulp in front of her.

"Sorry, ma'am. I won't do that again."

Vanessa would have fired many a crew member on the spot for that remark, but she'd decided not to let one remark from this woman ruin everything.

"Apology accepted. I'm Vanessa Widomski, the new Captain. I had a good read of your personal file from Captain Lansky. He thinks you have a good career ahead of you and I agree. If you're here to sign up and not just make tasteless jokes, I have this for you."

She reached over and handed her a letter.

"That's a letter from the New London Merchant Marine Corporation officially giving you the rank of Warrant Officer. You'll be my new Third Mate, in charge of safety and security procedures around this vessel. It's also got a voucher for the best tailor on this planet to make you a nice new blue uniform."

"Blue?"

"I'm not going to change everything round here, Mrs. Kumar. I'm not that stupid. I'm a Spacee just like you. Welcome to *Tulyar.*"

Acknowledgements

Thank you to Gavin, for the images.